To Siddhi,
who loves the snow.
— SB

To Priyanka Varun Sharma,
Jenica Sharma and Gabriel.
— EC

Text copyright © 2020 by Saumiya Balasubramaniam
Illustrations copyright © 2020 by Eva Campbell
Published in Canada and the USA in 2020 by Groundwood Books

Groundwood Books / House of Anansi Press
groundwoodbooks.com

We gratefully acknowledge for their financial support of our publishing
program the Canada Council for the Arts, the Ontario Arts Council and
the Government of Canada.

Library and Archives Canada Cataloguing in Publication
Title: Two drops of brown in a cloud of white / Saumiya Balasubramaniam ;
pictures by Eva Campbell.
Names: Balasubramaniam, Saumiya, author. | Campbell, Eva, illustrator.
Identifiers: Canadiana (print) 20190224584 | Canadiana (ebook) 20190224592 |
ISBN 9781773062587 (hardcover) | ISBN 9781773062594 (EPUB) |
ISBN 9781773063010 (Kindle)
Classification: LCC PS8603.A47 T96 2020 | DDC jC813/.6—dc23

The illustrations were done in oil and pastel on canvas.
Design by Michael Solomon
Printed and bound in China

Canada Council   Conseil des Arts
for the Arts   du Canada

ONTARIO ARTS COUNCIL
CONSEIL DES ARTS DE L'ONTARIO
an Ontario government agency
un organisme du gouvernement de l'Ontario

With the participation of the Government of Canada
Avec la participation du gouvernement du Canada | Canadä

FSC MIX
Paper from
responsible sources
www.fsc.org   FSC® C144853

Two Drops
of Brown
in a Cloud of
White

Saumiya Balasubramaniam · Eva Campbell

Groundwood Books
House of Anansi Press
Toronto Berkeley

ON A GRAY afternoon in December,
Ma and I walk home from school.

Well, she walks. I glide!

"Watch out for black ice,"
says Ma, and grabs my hand.
We walk around the icy patch.

I let go of her grip. Ma raises
her brows. Her brown eyes
grow big.

"Do as you like," she says,
and steps into giant footprints
ready-made in the snow.

I make new ones of my own.

I pack some snow. Looks — yummm
— like vanilla ice cream.

"So cold," says Ma. "And so white. I
can't wait for the sun to come out." She
tucks her chin into her royal-blue scarf.

Ma likes the sun. And she *loves* colors. I like her colors, especially when the diamond on her nose scatters the sun into violet, indigo, blue, green, yellow, orange and red.

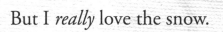

But I *really* love the snow.

"So much snow," says Ma. "So monochromatic."

"Mono crow what?"

"Monochromatic," says Ma. "Only one color. Only white."

"Too bad," I say. "I see the cozy gray of Kitty's tail curled up on that cloud." I point to the sky. "And the bright blue of her eyes!"

Ma looks up. A smile sneaks around the corners of her lips. A blue-green sparkle shimmers on her nose.

"I miss the green of palm
trees back home," she says.

"This is home!" I mutter.

We walk along. Ice crunches beneath our feet.
We see Priya and her grandma across the
street. Grandma usually waves or scurries over
to chat, but not today. Her chin is tucked into
her neck.
A sudden gust of wind blows. Priya almost
disappears behind a curtain of snow.

A maple leaf cartwheels in the air,
then hops onto my purple mitten.

"Oh, these dry brown leaves," says
Ma. "Like skeletons."

Leaf skeletons? I think to myself.

"Brown like maple syrup, Ma." I put
the leaf in my pocket.

Then I scoop up some snow and
toss it up to Kitty.
"See, see," I say, twirling under the
flakes. "Snow fireworks!"

"Let's go," says Ma, and grabs
my hand again.
New snow starts to fall.

I rush ahead and stick out my tongue.
"Now you try," I say to Ma.

She sticks out her tongue, then quickly
pulls it back in, like a gecko.

There is snow on snow everywhere — snow hats on birdhouses, snow hills on cars and rooftops.

I trace the shape of an S
on the sidewalk snow.
"S for snow?" says Ma.

"S for sun!" I say.

Ma hugs me tight.
"When the sun comes out,
everything will look so shiny
and bright!" she says.

"I see big brown eyes!" I say.

"Brown like syrup," says Ma. "I see home. I see two drops of brown in a cloud of white."